For Jean

Library of Congress Cataloging-in-Publication Data

Reader, Dennis, 1927–
I Want One!/Dennis Reader.
p.   cm.
"First published in Great Britain
by Walker Books Ltd."—T.p. verso.
Summary: Having acquired an assortment of exotic animals
by screaming until his parents get him what he wants,
Boris one day receives a just reward for his final scream.
ISBN 0-8249-8442-0 : $12.95
[1. Selfishness—Fiction.] I. Title.
P27.R235241aaw   1990
[E]—dc20   89-39899
                          CIP
                          AC

First published in the United States by
Ideals Publishing Corporation
Nelson Place at Elm Hill Pike
Nashville, Tennessee 37214
Copyright © 1990 by Dennis Reader
First published in Great Britain by
Walker Books Ltd., London, England
Printed and bound by L.E.G.O., Vicenza, Italy

ISBN 0-8249-8442-0

I WANT ONE! I WANT ONE! I WANT ONE!

Dennis Reader

IDEALS CHILDREN'S BOOKS
Nashville, Tennessee

There was once a boy named Boris who had nearly
everything he wanted. His mother and father gave him

. . . until, of course, he got it.

Then one day a new boy moved into the house next door. The boy's father was a famous explorer.

He came back from one trip with a beautiful, bouncing kangaroo—all the way from Australia.

Boris didn't have a beautiful, bouncing kangaroo.
So he screamed very loudly, "I want one!"

. . . until his parents trekked off across the world

and captured the biggest, bounciest kangaroo
in the whole of the Australian bush country.

The next time the explorer came home, he brought
a sleek and slithery giant anaconda all the way
from Peru.

Boris didn't have an anaconda of any kind,
so he screamed very loudly, "I want one!"

So his mother and father had to go off into the
jungle and catch the sleekest, slitheriest, most

enormous giant anaconda they could find.
It took them a week to wrestle it out of the river.

Then one morning the explorer came home with the most extraordinary present of all.

It came in a huge wooden crate stamped "YETI"— all the way from the Himalayas. Boris didn't know what a yeti was; but whatever it was, he didn't have one.

So he screamed very, very loudly, "I want one!"

"One what, dear?" asked his mother.

"A yeti!" screamed Boris.

"Oh no," sighed Boris's father, "here we go again."

Boris's mother and father put on their lined
parkas, wooly mittens, and best snow boots
and set off for the Himalaya Mountains.

Yetis aren't as easy to find as kangaroos or giant
anacondas, so it took Boris's mother and father
a long time to track one down.

Finally, though, with the help of a delicious
homemade cherry cake, they succeeded.

For a while, Boris had everything he wanted.
But then he grew bored with the yeti, just
as he'd grown bored with everything else.

The yeti grew bored with Boris too. So did the
kangaroo and the anaconda—especially when
they saw the fun and games the animals were
having next door. Boris saw this as well.

He frowned.

His face turned purple.

Then he screamed very loudly—louder than ever before— "I WANT TO PLAY A GAME!"

Smiling, the yeti put his arms around Boris.
The anaconda slithered under Boris's feet.
Then, very gently, the yeti picked Boris up and . . .

popped him into the anaconda's mouth.

"Boris is very quiet," said his mother. "I think that he finally must have gotten what he really wanted."

"Good," said Boris's father. "Maybe now *we'll* get
a little peace and quiet!"